THE SECRETS OF DROON

The Mask of Maliban

by Tony Abbott
Illustrated by Tim Jessell

A
LITTLE APPLE
PAPERBACK

SCHOLASTIC INC.
New York Toronto London Auckland Sydney
Mexico City New Delhi Hong Kong Buenos Aires

For Lucy and Jane,
May the power be yours forever

For more information about the continuing saga of Droon,
please visit Tony Abbott's website at
www.tonyabbottbooks.com

Book design by Dawn Adelman

ISBN 0-439-30606-X

12 11 10 9 8 7 6 5 4 3 2 1   1 2 3 4 5 6/0

Printed in the U.S.A.   40
First Scholastic printing, October 2001

Contents

1. A Little Extra Help   1

2. Mountain of the Firefrogs   17

3. In the City of Magic   28

4. Hob, the Impish Imp!   43

5. A Great Idea?   55

6. What the Evil Ones Are Wearing   64

7. The Magic in the Mask   77

8. The Big Chase   88

9. Welcome to the Dark Lands!   98

10. The End of Tortu's Tail   109

One

A Little Extra Help

"Ahhh!" screamed Eric Hinkle as he raced down the empty hallway at school.

He was running because he was being chased.

By hundreds of tiny green birds.

Quawk! Eeeep! Cheeeeep!

Eric knew these were no ordinary birds chasing him. They had sharp green wings and stubby pink beaks. And they came from another world.

The magical world of Droon.

Kraw! Kraw!

The birds zipped and swooped and fluttered and flitted up to the ceiling lights. Then they dived for his head, screeching all the way.

The amazing part was that he — Eric Hinkle, regular kid — had made the birds appear!

Quawk-awk-awk —

Out of breath, Eric slid into Mrs. Michaels's classroom and tumbled behind a desk.

He searched his memory to find what he had done wrong. Earlier that day, he had arranged with Mrs. Michaels to get extra math help. She said they could do it during last period when the rest of the school was in assembly.

Then at the end of the day as he headed

to her classroom, a mysterious word had popped into his head, just like that.

Topa-popa-snabbo.

"That's it!" Eric groaned to himself. "I shouldn't have said that word!"

But he had said it.

And suddenly — *quawk!* — birds were everywhere. They chased him down the hall. And now they were all over Mrs. Michaels's classroom. And they just kept coming — more and more and more of them!

"Get away!" he cried. Shielding his face with one arm, he swatted them away with the other, when another word popped into his head.

"Ya-ya-boko-mesh! I mean, huh — ?"

Kkkk — blam!

His fingers shot out a sudden spray of blue sparks and — *poomf!* — the birds vanished. All of them. As if they had never been there at all.

Eric slumped to the floor, exhausted. "What is going on? I mean, I can make stuff appear. I have these sparks coming out of my fingers. And I'm even having, sort of, visions!"

Yes, visions. That was another thing.

For several days he had found himself seeing and hearing things that were happening somewhere else. It was truly weird. Now sitting on the classroom floor, he tried to make it happen again.

He closed his eyes.

Suddenly, light flashed in his head, and he "saw" Mrs. Michaels pulling open a door somewhere in the school.

He opened his eyes and — *poof!* — she was gone. A vision.

Eric smiled to himself and said aloud

what he'd been thinking. "I have . . . magical powers."

He remembered exactly when he got the powers, too. It was on his last visit to Droon. He had been thrown into a deep cavern by a whispering evil spirit named Om.

To save Eric, his friend Princess Keeah had directed a blast of blue wizard light at him. It had saved him, all right. But it had done something else, too. Keeah's light had entered into him, filling him with its glow.

She didn't know it, but his fingers had been sparking ever since. Well, almost ever since.

Eric never knew when he would have the powers. In fact, every time he tried to show his friends Neal and Julie, his hands turned normal again. No sparks. No powers. No nothing.

"What if my powers go away when I tell people?" he asked himself. "I mean, I like being . . . Eric Hinkle . . . kid wizard!"

He laughed. Whirling around, he pointed his fingers at some blackboard erasers on the desk, and a new word came to him.

"Lev . . . ta . . . lem!"

Amazed, Eric watched as a stream of sparks left his fingertips and drifted over to the erasers. The erasers wobbled once, then rose from the desk.

"I'm doing it!" he cried. "I'm doing it —"

The door squeaked.

"Oh, no!" He shoved his hands in his pockets, and the erasers crashed to the floor in a puff of dust.

Mrs. Michaels entered the room. She started to cough. "My goodness, Eric, what are you doing?" She waved the chalk dust away from her face.

"Sorry, Mrs. Michaels. I'm here for the

extra help we talked about." He put the erasers back on the desk.

"Then let's get started, shall we?"

For the next thirty minutes, Mrs. Michaels went over math problems while Eric did his best to hide his sparking fingertips.

"I think I understand the problems now," he said finally.

She smiled. "You can always get extra help when you're having trouble with something."

"Extra help. I sure need that." What Eric really needed was extra help controlling his powers.

"Next time, don't keep it such a secret."

"No secrets," he said. "Right. Got it."

He suddenly felt bad about not telling Julie and Neal about what was happening to him.

Friends don't keep secrets from friends.

Brrrinnng! The final school bell rang. Eric thanked Mrs. Michaels, grabbed his books, then jumped into the hallway. It was already crowded with kids coming back from the assembly.

"Eric!" called a loud voice. "Today's the day!"

He turned to see Julie and Neal trotting toward him. He grinned. "The day for what?"

Neal grabbed Eric's arm and tugged him close to the lockers. "The three of us are going back to you-know-where!"

"Really?" said Eric. "Today? Are you sure?"

Julie laughed. "Keeah said our dreams tell us when we're needed in Droon, right? Well, it was so hot in the auditorium —"

"And the assembly took forever," said Neal.

"—that we both fell asleep, and guess

what?" said Julie. "We both dreamed of the same creature! He was all furry with red and yellow spots. He was very cute."

"But mostly weird," Neal added, making a face. "And Droon is the only place with weird creatures . . . besides the mall, I mean!"

Eric laughed. "That's for sure."

After their bus had been called, they left the school, got on the bus, and plopped down in their seats.

"We figure we're being called back for a special mission," said Julie. "I wonder what Galen's got cooking up for us this time!"

Galen Longbeard was the very old and very powerful first wizard of Droon. Eric wondered what Galen would say if he knew that Eric had powers, too. Would he make him give them up?

Eric decided not to tell anyone his secret until he could learn more. And the only place to do that was Droon.

The bus started up and pulled onto the street.

"I can't wait to see Keeah again," said Julie. "And Max, of course. He's so funny!"

Neal nodded. "But there are some folks who aren't so funny. Lord Sparr, for instance. Yuck."

Lord Sparr.

Just the name made the kids shiver. Sparr was a sorcerer who wanted to take over all of Droon. He would have succeeded, too, but Keeah had turned his own wicked creation, the Golden Wasp, against him. Sparr had been stung by it.

Since then, people told stories about the terrible monster Sparr had become. The kids were sure they had seen him recently. If it was him, "monster" was certainly the right word. Instead of a man with a black cloak and fins behind his ears, Sparr was all dark and scaly with a red snout and long teeth. Yep, "monster" was the word.

Eric shivered for another reason, too. He was remembering what the spirit Om had whispered.

He said Eric would help Sparr. *Help him!*

Just then, the bus stopped at Eric's house.

"To the basement!" he cried.

They scrambled into his house and headed down to the basement. Moving some boxes, they revealed a small door under the stairs.

"Last one in is a rotten egg," said Eric.

"Wait!" Neal froze. "Did you say . . . egg? Egg is food. Food is good. I'm suddenly hungry!"

"Neal!" said Julie, rolling her eyes.

Eric was about to say that there was a box of doughnuts in the kitchen when another word popped into his head and right out of his mouth.

"*Bubb-zee-doo* —"

Neal looked puzzled. "Is that a new kind of snack food?"

Splop! A jelly doughnut — a fat, powdery, jelly-filled doughnut — appeared behind Neal's head. Another popped up behind Julie's head.

Soon, more and more of them appeared. The doughnuts began to spin in circles.

Eric's eyes bugged out. "How about we catch a meal in Droon? Now!" He pushed his friends into the closet before they could see anything.

"Somebody wants to get there fast!" said Julie as Eric slammed the door behind them.

"I sure do," said Eric. "Everybody ready?"

He flicked off the ceiling light.

The closet went dark, then — *whoosh!* — the cold gray floor vanished. In its place shimmered the rainbow-colored staircase to Droon.

"This is my favorite thing," said Julie excitedly. "I mean, where else besides Droon can life be so . . . magical?"

Eric thought about the doughnuts flying around his basement and smiled. "Right. Where else?"

Together, the three friends climbed down the stairs. Lower and lower they went. But with every step, dark shadows fell over the staircase.

"I know the stairs always lead to someplace new," said Neal. "But let me be the first to say it's blacker than night down there. I just hope it's not a trap set by Lord Sparr."

The steps wound down into total darkness.

"Or by some new creepy villain," added Julie.

Crunch! The ground was rough under their shoes.

"We're at the bottom," said Eric. "We must be in a tunnel — holy cow! — what's that?"

Splop! Splop! There was a strange sound and a flash of green. Then out of the distance came a rolling, hopping, boiling swarm of creatures.

Splop! They looked like frogs but had big purple eyes and were as large as cats.

Their skins were blazing with bright green flames that lit the tunnel with a fantastic glow.

"Back up the stairs!" yelled Julie.

Eric glanced behind them. "Too late. They're fading. We'll find them when it's time to go home."

"But I want to go home now!" cried Neal.

They took another look at the frogs bounding wildly at them. And for the second time that day, Eric started to scream.

Two

Mountain of the Firefrogs

Eric was still screaming — "Ahhh!" — when a voice shouted from the darkness. "STOP!"

The army of fiery green creatures slid to a halt inches from the kids. Their tongues flicked in and out.

"Eric? Julie? Neal?" said a soft voice from the shadows. "Is that . . . *you?*"

The kids peered into the gloom and

saw a young girl in a blue tunic walking toward them.

"Princess Keeah!" Julie exclaimed.

"That's me!" said Keeah, smiling in the glow of the frogs. Her long blond hair was encircled by a golden crown. "I'm so happy to see you!"

"We had to come," Neal said. "We dreamed of a furry little dude with yellow and red spots —"

"His name is Hob!" chirped a tiny voice.

Scrambling up the tunnel wall was Max, the spider troll. He had eight twitching legs and a plump grinning face. "Hob is the very imp we're searching for," Max said. "He escaped his mountain prison. Now you can help us find him!"

"Too bad these tunnels are empty," said Keeah. "Firefrogs, let's report to Galen at once."

The frogs hopped about excitedly. Tiny flames sprayed off their heads as they followed Keeah and the children upward through the tunnels.

"In my dream, Hob looked sort of cute and fuzzy," said Julie. "Is he really so bad?"

Max scurried alongside. "He wasn't always bad. Hob was famous as a maker of masks."

"Masks?" said Eric. "What kind of masks?"

"Like Halloween masks?" asked Neal.

The princess shook her head. "Hob made masks for the royal theater of Jaffa City. He was the finest mask maker in all of Droon."

"Until five years ago," the spider troll added. "That's when Hob began carving magical symbols on his masks. Magical symbols from the evil empire of Goll!"

At that moment the tunnels opened out

onto a mountaintop in broad daylight. On the mountain was a small village of squat green buildings.

"Hob's masks suddenly had powers," Keeah went on. "So Galen banished him to this mountain, where he was watched over by the firefrogs."

Banished? thought Eric. *For having powers? Will I be banished, too?*

In the center of the village stood a tall man in a blue cloak. His long white beard whirled in the wind sweeping across the mountain.

It was the great wizard Galen.

Galen turned sharply, greeting the children with a hasty smile. He glanced a second time at Eric, his old face tense and gray, as if he were about to say something.

Eric wondered if Galen sensed his powers.

But the wizard turned to Keeah. "I see

in your face that Hob is gone. Now the trouble begins!"

Neal raised his hand. "Could this have anything to do with, you know, nasty old Sparr?"

"Sparr!" Galen's eyes flashed. "Sparr does not meddle with such imps as Hob. No, since Sparr was stung by the Wasp, he is weak, hiding away many miles from here. Look!"

From a pocket deep inside his cloak the wizard took out a small mirror. It was a tiny version of the large magic mirror Galen kept in his tower. Using it, he could see across all of Droon.

"I see him, even now," Galen said, tracing his finger over the foggy surface of the glass.

Eric peeked at the mirror, but saw nothing. He saw Keeah squinting at the mirror, too.

"Sparr is in his volcano palace on the far side of his Dark Lands," said Galen. "We need not worry about him today."

Neal grinned. "Then I can relax. A day without old fish fins is a day of fun!"

"Do not be so sure," said the wizard. "Hob has his own mischief to do. And we must find out what. Firefrogs, which of you saw Hob last?"

One by one the frogs quieted and stepped aside. In their midst crouched a tiny frog, her purple eyes bulging with worry.

"Forgive me, Sir Galen!" she warbled. "It was my first day. Hob was too clever for me!"

Galen's stern expression remained for a moment, then softened. He knelt next to the tiny frog. "Now, now, my little friend," he said. "I'm sure you'll grow into a fine watcher one day. For now, just tell me what happened."

The creature sniffled once, then began to speak. "Hob said he was hungry. He asked for a bowl of stew. So I gave him one."

"A bowl? A bowl!" said the wizard. "Yes, I begin to see. What happened next?"

"Before I could take it back, Hob shaped the bowl into a mask. It was like the head of a bird."

"A bird," said Galen, stroking his chin. "Certainly a good choice. What did Hob do then?"

"He made circles and lines all over the mask," the frog whimpered. "Strange they were! And when he put on the mask he flew right out of the village! And he boasted he was going to make another mask, even better!"

"Another?" questioned the wizard. "For whom?"

"Someone named Prince Maliban —"

"A minor spell caster," said Galen. "I've heard of him. Like many others, he saw his chance for fame when Sparr went into hiding!"

"He lives now in Tortu," said the frog.

"Tortu!" Galen boomed, bolting to his feet. "The city of the turtle! Oh, a terrible den of dark spells, magic, and mystery, Tortu is! A city of evil and danger!"

"Evil? Danger?" said Neal, gulping loudly. "Guess where we must be going?"

The wizard chuckled. "Right you are, Neal. Now, Keeah . . ." The wizard scanned the distant horizon. "Tortu is east of the Kubar River, on the Thousand Mile Plains, near the pink mountains of Saleef. Do the honors, if you will."

"Certainly!" said the princess.

Eric watched closely as Keeah shut her eyes and made a swirling motion with her hands. A funnel of blue air twinkled up around them.

It suddenly felt as if they were moving.

An instant later — *poomf!* — the light was gone. They were standing at the foot of a hill on the edge of a great rolling plain. The sun shone down on miles and miles of tall grass. Far in the distance was a range of pink-topped mountains.

"Cool," said Neal. "Nonstop express to . . . to . . . hey, I don't see any city of evil and danger. Not that I'm complaining, but Galen, sir, did you get the directions wrong?"

"My master is never wrong!" chirped Max. "And the proof is there —"

Thwump! Thwump!

The earth rumbled beneath their feet.

"The city of Tortu," said Galen. "It's coming!"

Eric frowned. "The city is . . . *coming?*"

Then, over the crest of a hill behind them came an enormous brown foot. *Thwump!* It planted itself heavily on the earth. Then another foot reached over. *Thwump!*

Finally, a giant drooping head, with two huge blinking eyes, bobbed up over the hill.

"A . . . a . . . turtle!" gasped Julie, her mouth dropping open. "A giant, giant, *giant* turtle!"

And soaring up from the turtle's vast shell was an entire city of towers, walls, turrets, and bridges.

"Behold Tortu!" said Galen. "City of magic!"

Three

In the City of Magic

Thwump! Thwump!

The great glum head of the turtle bobbed up and down as each foot slammed the plains, driving the city closer and closer to them.

"It's . . . big . . ." Neal mumbled. "Real big."

The shell, thick and polished and brown, was as wide and long as ten football fields.

Each foot was larger than their school.

The creature's head was as big as an office building, and its two sleepy eyes were the size of satellite dishes. Soon the kids were in its shadow.

"This is so awesome," said Eric, looking up.

Julie gaped at the underside of the shell. "Awesome, yes, but how do we get up there?"

"Max, if you please?" said Galen with a smile.

"At your service, master." Max twitched his eight legs rapidly and wove a ladder of the strongest spider silk. "This should do it."

With a single mighty throw, Galen tossed the ladder up. It hooked on the turtle's shell.

"Grab hold," shouted Keeah. "And up we go!"

Before the turtle lurched forward, they leaped to the ladder and climbed all the way to the top.

Clambering over the side of the shell, they saw a crowded city of towers and bridges, of clustered houses, of gates and turrets and arches and rooftops.

But the black walls of a palace rose up high above the rest.

"The palace, no doubt, of this fellow Maliban," said Galen as they approached an opening in the walls.

"Within this city we will find only enemies," said Max. "I can feel it."

"Well said, my friend," said Galen. "Tortu carries the worst of the worst on its back. Magic thieves, spell mongers, and common street magicians. They buy and sell — and make and steal — magic. Be watchful, everyone!"

They passed under the archway and

soon were in the middle of a lively mar-
ketplace. The sun shone through bright-
colored canopies, casting fantastic shadows
on the turtle's shell.

Julie smiled. "It's like the mall of Droon!"

"The evil mall of Droon," said Neal.
"Look at those guys." He pointed to a band
of large, three-legged men in dirty rags and
eyepatches. They were browsing at a stall
displaying flaming swords.

"Three-legged hoolifans," said Max, his
eyes bulging. "They are magic thieves.
They rob caravans of potions and spells.
Terrible brutes!"

"Never mind them," said Galen. "Look
there."

A strange tall figure in a dark green robe
and hood peered around a nearby corner.
Another ducked into the shadow of a
doorway. Reddish eyes gleamed from the
depths of their hoods.

"Not your typical shoppers," said Julie.

"They are not shopping," said Galen. "If I am right, they are spies for Prince Maliban. I especially do not like the way their eyes follow us so closely. Let us move on."

The deeper they went into the market, the more the streets twisted and curved.

Passing through one alley, they saw an old man sitting cross-legged in his stall. His gray beard was wrapped around him like a sweater.

Before him was a carpet hovering in the air.

"Rugs crafted by Pasha himself, stolen while he slept," the man called out. "Easy to fly. No experience necessary!"

"Flying carpets," said Neal. "I want one —"

Eric and Julie pulled him along. In the next shop was what looked like a large blue cat. The cat puffed on a pipe and blew smoke rings that looked like the faces of those who passed by.

"Spell casters," whispered Galen. "Charm stealers. Street conjurors. Pah! Every sort of common magic thief and swindler is in Tortu!"

The wizard swept angrily through the streets, his eyes straining, his ears listening for any sound of the imp Hob at work.

Before long they came to a place where the market split into two narrow but crowded alleys.

"Now we must spread out and be careful," the wizard said. "Tortu is a dangerous place for those who don't have evil on their minds. We must find Hob and be quick about it!"

Galen darted off down the alley to the right, with Max scurrying nervously by his side.

"Let's be careful not to run into any of

Maliban's green-hooded spies," said Keeah, looking into the crowds. "They scare me."

Slowly they stepped into the crowded alley.

Passing a stall filled with giant brown urns of water, Neal nudged Eric in the arm. "I just heard somebody say there's a bake-shop down here somewhere. Maybe Hob's hungry after flying all the way here. I'll check it out."

"Stay close," said Eric. He watched Neal sniff the air, then make a beeline to a nearby shop.

Eric was about to join Julie and Keeah when sunlight flickered in his face. He closed his eyes. In that moment, he saw something.

A tail. With sharp spikes running down it.

When Eric opened his eyes again,

something was moving in the small space between two shops.

"Hel-l-l-lp . . . me-e-e-e-e!" said a voice.

"Who's in there?" Eric said. "Are you okay?"

"Hel-l-l-lp me-e-e-e-e!" was the reply.

"Wait!" Eric shouted.

Something dark and thick and covered with scales slithered away between the walls.

Suddenly, Eric's hands felt hot. He looked down to see them sparking more brightly than they ever had before. "Whoa, cool —"

When he looked back, whatever it was that he had seen was gone.

And his hands were normal again.

"Man, this is nuts. I can't control this at all!"

He found Julie and Keeah in the street

and told them what he had seen. "It was dark and creepy and had a tail with spiky spikes all over it."

"Eeew," said Julie, making a face. "Tortu is starting to scare me. That thing didn't attack you, did it?"

Eric shook his head. "No. In fact, I think it wanted me to help it somehow. Then it disappeared."

"Maybe we'll see it again," said the princess. "In the meantime, let's keep an eye out for Hob."

They pressed farther down the alley, listening for the sounds of the mask maker at work.

Eric turned to the princess. "Keeah? I wanted to ask you. What does it feel like to use your powers?"

"I've always wondered that, too," said Julie.

Keeah smiled. "First, I go to a quiet

place in my mind that Galen taught me about. It's like a little room, all my own. Only when I concentrate can I really control my powers. If I'm upset or scared, I can make mistakes. Big mistakes."

"No control," said Eric. "I know what you mean. I feel the same way. I mean, about other stuff —"

"Whoa!" Neal was suddenly racing toward them, looking scared.

"What's the matter?" said Eric. "Couldn't find the bakeshop?"

Neal shook his head frantically. "Turned out to be a *snake* shop. But that's not the worst part. The worst part is . . . them!"

Two young girls with orange faces, long silky gowns, and high turbans on their heads burst from the snake shop. They giggled and pointed at Neal. "Yellow hair! Oooh!" They raced over.

"Hide me!" Neal squealed. "They keep

touching my hair. Now I know what it feels like to be a pop star. And I don't like it!"

Neal jumped behind Julie, tripped over a big urn of water, and slid behind a curtain. The two girls flew past the shop. But the big urn teetered and wobbled and pitched and then tipped over.

Splash! Pink water spilled everywhere.

"Hey!" growled the shop owner, a man with a tiny head nearly covered with blue hair. "That's magic water from the Kubar River. It cures illness! Now I gotta mop it up!" He stormed off.

"Does it cure Nealness?" Julie asked, looking at the pink water spilling over her sneakers. "My shoes are all wet!"

Neal peeked out from behind the curtain. "Look at it this way. At least your shoes won't get a cold."

"No, but I will. My feet are soaked —"

"Hey, you, out of the way!" boomed a voice.

Keeah jumped aside as a large wooden cart rumbled up the alley, nearly running her over.

Marching on each side of the cart were six green-hooded guards. Beneath their hoods their red eyes blazed.

"Magic boots for Prince Maliban!" shouted the driver. In the back of the cart were dozens of finely made velvet boots of different colors.

"Make way to the palace!" said another guard, pushing Julie away roughly. When he did, a pair of green boots bounced out of the cart.

"Hey, a pair of your boots fell out," said Julie.

"Be gone!" the guard snapped, glaring

at her with his deep red eyes. "We're on our way to the palace!"

"Green meanie," she whispered. "You don't have to be so rude!"

The cart wound away through the alley.

Eric picked up the boots. "Look, Julie, it's almost like they knew your sneakers were wet."

Julie took off her shoes and put on the boots. "Magic boots, huh? I wonder what they do."

Neal grinned. "Keep your feet magically dry?"

"Something isn't right here," said Keeah, still watching the cart on its way to the palace. "Why does Maliban want magic boots?"

"Maybe he likes to dance," said Neal.

Keeah shook her head. "Let's just find Hob."

But at that moment, Max came swinging down from the rooftop above, huffing and puffing and squealing and squeaking.

"Hob!" he said. "Hob, my friends! Hob! We found him! And his mask! Follow me at once!"

H☉b, the Impish Imp!

Max led the children quickly through one crowded alley after another. Then they heard it.

Tap . . . tap. Clink . . . clink.

"Up there!" Max chirped, pointing to a small two-story building just ahead of them. "It's Hob at work over the basket shop! Galen is already there!"

The spider troll scampered up the wall

while the kids raced up a set of stairs and across the roof.

They entered the upper floor by slipping through a small window. In the dim light, they spotted the wizard. He put a finger to his lips and motioned them over to a wall of baskets.

Tap . . . tap.

"Look behind here." Smiling, Galen pushed a basket aside. Light flickered out from behind it.

Keeah peered in, then gasped. "It's Hob! In his workshop. Everyone, look!"

Inside was a small room with a workbench in the center. The bench was piled high with tools and lit by thick candles. Hunched over the bench was what appeared to be a large, spotted dog.

"The imp himself," whispered Max. "Imps are usually trouble and none more so than Hob!"

"But he's so cute!" said Julie.

Hob *was* cute in a way. Thick spotted fur covered him from snout to curly tail. He sported short rear legs, but his front paws were long and slender, almost like hands, and always moving.

The imp gulped and snorted and sang as he worked. "Hob, Hob, good at his job! Good at his task, to make a mask. Make a mask as fine as he can. A magic mask for Maliban!"

Hob seemed a fuzzy ball of energy. He hunched over the bench for a moment, then zipped up to the highest shelf, grabbed a tool, and leaped back to his work again.

But it was when he left the bench that everyone saw what he was working on.

A terrifying golden face. A mask of terror.

Jutting out the front were the jaws and

teeth of an angry beast. Red jewels were its eyes. Its fangs were gold, hammered as sharp as knives.

With one curious tool, Hob carved a series of multicolored symbols onto the edges of the mask. When he finished, the mask began to glow a deep red.

"This mask of Hob is no mere trinket," whispered Galen. "This is a mask of . . . dark power!"

"Who *is* Prince Maliban?" Keeah wondered.

Galen could wait no longer. Bursting through the wall of baskets, he sprang into the workshop.

"Hob!" he cried. "We have found you!"

The imp froze where he sat. His tools clattered to the floor. "Hob knows that voice. Hob doesn't like that voice. That voice — is Galen's!"

He whirled around on his rear legs, his

front paws clutching the mask before him. "Galen and his troop of junior wizards! But Hob doesn't want to go back to the firefrog mountain. No, no!"

"We shall take you," said the wizard. "But first, tell us. Where did you learn these magical symbols?"

The imp chuckled darkly. "In the forests of Jabar-loo," he said, his eyes lighting up. "Hob saw palaces there. Palaces of Goll!"

"Goll was destroyed centuries ago," Galen snapped. "I cast the first flame onto the evil empire myself. Goll is nothing but broken stones now."

"And yet Hob felt their power!" he said, trembling with excitement. "Hob learned Goll's magic words. They fill Hob's masks with power!"

Keeah stepped forward. "Why does Maliban want a mask with such powerful magic?"

Hob buffed the golden mask with his furry arm. "Well . . . he can't go around with his face like that, can he?"

"What's wrong with his face?" asked Eric.

Hob chuckled. "Perhaps you'll find out! Now, Maliban needs his mask. Hob must go. Bye!"

Squealing with delight, he leaped through the window and out into the market.

"After him!" shouted Keeah.

Eric and Neal jumped out the window and across the roof to the top of the next shop.

"He's in the alley!" Julie shouted behind them.

Galen and Max scrambled down to the street, but Hob flashed by one stall and grabbed a pawful of tiny silver stars and moons. He tossed them at Galen. They began buzzing around the wizard's head like a swarm of bees.

"Just a little magic of Tortu!" the imp said.

While Max and Galen swatted the buzzing stars and moons away, Hob chuckled merrily and disappeared into an alley.

"Oh, no you don't!" cried Keeah. "Stop him!"

As if on a tightrope, Eric scampered across a balcony ledge and slid down an awning to the ground. "I'm coming!" he said. "I'm —"

Suddenly, he heard it again. The strange voice —

"Hel-l-l-lp me-e-e-e!"

Eric screeched to a stop, swung his head both ways, then darted into an alley between a wand maker's stand and a flying-lizard shop.

The sun was beginning to set and the alley was darkened by blue shadows. Eric ran halfway to the end, then stopped.

The voices of his friends seemed to fade. Then he saw it. Clutching the wall at the corner was what looked like a hand, except it wasn't a hand. It was a claw, shriveled and twisted with thick curved tips instead of fingers.

"Oh, my gosh," Eric mumbled.

The skin on the claw was black and scaly, but with pale blotches all over it. It was a terrible thing to see. And only one word came into Eric's head.

It wasn't a Droon word.

It was a plain old Upper-World word. *Monster.*

Then, as Eric watched, the claw whipped around the corner, carving lines into the stone of the building. There was a brief slithering noise, then all was quiet.

"Holy cow," whispered Eric.

Julie darted into the alley. "Eric, come on, we need you!"

Eric ran back to his friends and saw Hob clambering up an awning. The imp lurched across another roof, still clutching the golden mask.

"Hob runs away," the imp squealed. "He lives to run another day!" In a flash he was gone.

"We'll corner him in the next alley," said Keeah, who was still following the action from the rooftops. "Julie, jump up and grab my hand!"

Julie did jump toward Keeah. But instead of joining her — *boing!* — Julie leaped over the roof, over the building, and over the street, landing somewhere in the next block.

Eric and Neal nearly crashed into each other.

"Julie just jumped over the street!" said Eric.

"I guess we know what kind of magic boots they are," said Keeah.

"That was so cool!" said Neal. "I want boots like that!"

Boing! Julie bounced back to the street again. Her mouth was hanging open. "I just saw Hob. He's fast but I think I can catch him —"

Boing! She bounded over two more buildings, then back again. But when she landed —

"Halt!" The little street suddenly filled with Maliban's spies. They rushed to surround Julie.

"Green meanies!" said Neal, racing down the street with Eric. "You leave Julie alone."

The spies glared at them. "This girl has

magic. Magic goes to Maliban. We take her to Maliban!"

"I don't think so!" yelled Eric. He started running at the spies. His hands felt hot and he didn't care who saw them. He didn't care what happened. They were trying to take Julie away.

"Eric, no!" said Keeah.

But he only ran faster at the tall men, thrust out his hands, and aimed his fingers at them.

"Take that!" he yelled.

Five

A Great Idea?

"Take what?" growled one of the spies.

Eric stood there, flicking his fingers at the hooded men and watching as nothing happened.

His fingers were just fingers.

"Be gone!" said the guards. "Or face the anger of Maliban!"

The guards picked Julie up and whisked her away. In moments, she was lost in a crush of carts and wagons heading to the palace.

"What have I done?" Eric gasped, still staring at his hands. "I was going to stop those guys. With my powers!"

Keeah patted him on the shoulder. "Eric . . ."

"No, really!" he protested. "I have powers! I really do! At least, I did —"

"Hey, I know, pal," said Neal. "I wish I could do something, too. I'd love to zap those green meanies. But there are hundreds of them. We'd end up just as captured as Julie is. Maliban would probably lock all of us up in some smelly dungeon. With no food!"

Eric felt completely helpless. What if his powers were gone for good? What if Maliban hurt Julie? And all because he gave her the magic boots!

"What are we going to do?" he asked.

Keeah pulled them into a small space between two shops and stared out. Wagon after wagon rumbled to the palace. "The first thing I'm going to do is call Galen."

Neal laughed. "Call Galen? I didn't know you have cell phones in Droon!"

The princess smiled. "Galen just taught me this." She closed her eyes and went quiet. She frowned darkly, then began to nod to herself.

Eric poked his head out of the stall. One cart heaped high with floating carpets rolled by. It was driven by Maliban's guards. After it passed, the streets were quiet. No more carts went by.

Keeah opened her eyes. "I told Galen and Max everything."

Neal blinked. "You can talk to each other silently? That's so cool."

"Galen warned me there is very dark magic in Tortu," said Keeah. "And Hob has hidden himself somewhere. We are to go to the palace and find Julie. And we must do it quickly. . . . The turtle has turned."

"Turned?" said Neal. "Where is he heading?"

"Into the Dark Lands," she said.

Eric gasped. "The Dark Lands of Lord Sparr?"

Neal sighed. "Yes, my friend, we go to all the best places. Come on, then. I guess our first stop is the big black palace of Maliban the mystery man."

Carefully, they zigzagged through the passages to the center of Tortu. Soon, the market streets ended and there stood a high wall of black stone.

"Maliban's palace," said Eric.

"Correction," said Neal. "Maliban's scary, bad, evil palace of magic. And if you thought a few hooded guys were scary, check *them* out."

A wall of hooded guards stood at the door.

"We'll never get past them," said Eric. "They already know we're friends of Julie."

Keeah spun around. "And I see another problem. Neal, take a look. . . ."

Up the street came the two girls in turbans whom they had seen in the market. They were squealing and laughing to each other.

Neal jumped. "It's the giggle twins! Please don't let them touch my hair. Hide me!"

They dived into the nearest shop. In it were rows of magic cloaks and gowns, tall coned hats, and jeweled scarves. The two girls passed by.

"We're late," said the one dressed in pink, holding up a piece of paper. "Maliban will be angry. I have the black letter. Do you have the — ¿"

"Yes!" said the one in blue, tapping a leather pouch that hung at her side. "But where is our bodyguard? They're expecting three of us!"

"They're going to the palace," whispered Eric. "The black letter must be an invitation!"

"I suddenly have a great idea!" said Keeah. She jumped out of the shop, pulling Neal with her. "Oh, girls! Look who I've got here."

"What?" groaned Neal. "Oh, man —"

The two girls squealed when they saw him. "Cute! Yellow hair!" They ran to the shop.

But the moment they came near, Keeah said, *"Spindle . . . tres . . . flim!"*

The girls stopped in their tracks, giggled once — "hee-hee!" — and fainted.

"They'll wake in a few minutes," said Keeah, snatching the letter and the pouch.

"Giving us just enough time to take their places."

"Um . . . wait," said Neal. "Take their places? Is this your great idea? I mean, even including their bodyguard, how are two guys and a girl going to become two girls and a guy?"

"Simple," said Keeah, turning to the rows of rich clothes. "One of you will dress as a girl."

Both boys took a step backward.

"Not me," said Neal.

"Well, not me, either," said Eric.

Keeah sighed. "Julie's trapped in the palace."

"But it's impossible for me to go as a girl," Neal protested. "Because of my ears."

"What's wrong with your ears?" asked Eric.

"Nothing! That's just the point," said Neal. "Everybody knows girl ears are smaller than boy ears. And no offense, Eric, but your ears are more like girl ears than mine."

"I do not have girl ears!" said Eric, glancing into a nearby mirror. "Keeah, tell him."

"You do have cute ears," said the princess.

Neal's smile grew. "Besides, I'm perfect for the part of the bodyguard. I'm tall and cool-looking and mostly all muscles."

Neal pulled a blue gown off a rack and draped it over Eric's shoulder. "This one even matches your eyes. How about it . . . Erica?"

Eric stomped his foot and began to shout.

"I won't, I won't, I won't —"

Six

What the Evil Ones Are Wearing

"Are you sure this dress matches my eyes?" said Eric as he pulled the gown over his head.

"Yes," said Keeah, "and I'm borrowing it when we're done!"

Laughing, Neal wrapped a scarf high around Eric's head like a turban. "See, you're perfect for the part. You look exactly like a giggle twin."

Eric grumbled. "I'm only doing this for Julie, you know. Now let's find her."

Night was falling in the darkest part of the dark quarter of Tortu when the three friends left the shop. Lamps along the street swung gently as the turtle continued its journey.

The black palace loomed just ahead of them. Its steps were lined with green-hooded guards.

"Maliban's house of magic," said Neal. "Are we sure we're ready for this?"

"We don't have much choice," said Eric, glancing at his hands. They were normal. He wished they weren't.

"Start giggling," said Keeah.

"Hee-hee," said Eric, his voice quaking with fear. He led the way up the palace steps.

A guard at the door took the black letter

from Keeah. His red eyes scanned it. "The twin princesses of Samarindo!" he proclaimed. "Prince Maliban is expecting you. Enter, Princess Sarla!"

"That's me," squealed Keeah. "Tee-hee!"

"Enter, her sister, Princess Looma!"

"Tee-hee," squeaked Eric, swishing his gown.

"Enter, their servant . . . Doofus the Ugly!"

Neal started to choke. "Doo . . . Doo . . . Doofus the Ugly? Is he kidding? That's my name?"

Eric pulled Neal in past the guards. "It's like you said, pal, you're perfect for the part. Now don't forget to look ugly." Eric mussed up Neal's hair. "And watch your feet, you're stepping on my gown!"

Guards ushered them through the hallways.

Neal tried to walk hunched over.

"Should we make a break for it and find the dungeon?" he whispered.

"No," whispered Keeah. "Too risky."

"Besides," said Eric, "we don't know for sure what Maliban is up to. . . ."

Suddenly, Eric saw something in his mind. He saw a curtain. A bloodred curtain of thick velvet. It was rippling. And a terrible noise came from behind the curtain. *"Gggll . . . kkk . . ."*

It was as if someone — or something — was trying to speak. Then a claw, the same claw Eric had glimpsed in the market, stuck out from behind the curtain. A moment later, the vision was over.

Eric shook his head clear and marched ahead.

The guards led the children into an open courtyard. The floor of the yard was the turtle's polished shell. Though the sky above was moonless and growing darker, the air was warmed and lit by flaming torches hung from the walls.

But the children noticed none of this. Because in the center of the courtyard was a statue.

The statue was made of gleaming silver and shaped like a man clothed in long royal robes. It was nearly lifelike, except that its head was completely smooth. The only feature was a mouth, which was opened wide.

A sudden voice echoed out of it. "Welcome!"

"Um . . . Maliban is a statue?" whispered Eric.

"A shiny silver statue," said Neal, "that talks."

"Have you brought what I asked of you?" echoed the eerie voice.

The three kids looked at one another. Keeah felt the pouch at her side. "Oh!

Of course." To her surprise she reached in and removed a red ball the size of a base-ball.

It glowed warmly in her hand.

"The Ruby Orb of Doobesh!" said the statue. "Orb of wonder, Orb of enchantment. Hold it over your head and twirl it three times."

Keeah looked at Eric and Neal.

"Better do what he — I mean *it* — says," whispered Neal. "The meanies are all staring at us."

Keeah did as the statue commanded. Suddenly — *whizzz!* — the Orb shot out of her hand, circled the courtyard three times, and flew straight up into the air.

"Whoa!" said Eric. "I mean, tee-hee! How nice!"

"The Orb has a *special* purpose in the future of Droon," said the statue. "Now, behold!"

At that moment, guards entered the courtyard carrying all the objects the children had seen in the market. Those, and many more besides.

They brought in giant urns of water. Floating carpets. Colorful boots that jumped up and down. Spinning plates. Staffs of sparkling light. Swords that flew. Bubbling cauldrons. Books that spoke their words. Bells that jingled by themselves. Golden wands with tips of fire.

The guards piled these objects at the foot of the statue until there was a huge heap.

"Magic for Maliban!" shouted the guards.

And then came something else.

Two more guards marched in with a big brown sack. Something in the sack was squirming.

"A girl who knows magic!" said one of the guards. "She did a spell in the streets of Tortu!"

"Uh-oh," whispered Eric.

The guards emptied the sack. Julie tumbled out. She looked around in fear but saw only two strange girls and a hunched-over boy with messy hair. The guards held her tightly at one side of the statue.

"And now —" said the voice.

Boom! The doors burst open and there was a scampering of tiny feet. A furry creature scurried in and screeched to a stop before the statue.

"Whew! Never fear! Hob is here. Oh, the trouble he had! But with a little magic, Hob lost old Galen and his spider troll in the streets!"

"I hope they're not too lost," Neal whispered. "We're way outnumbered here."

"Let the magic begin!" boomed the voice.

Hob scampered to the statue and in one-two-three moves had set the golden mask over its head. "Nice, don't you think?"

The moment Hob jumped away, a thick red swirl of mist shot up from one of the magical objects heaped below. Then another. And another.

"It's working!" the statue's voice cried out.

Soon, the entire pile of magical objects was surrounded by a red wind, whirling like a small tornado around the statue.

Whoom! The dark air spun faster.

"Prepare to witness the greatest act of magic you have ever seen!" shouted the statue's voice. "I show you this to thank you for bringing me the Ruby Orb. You've done well . . . to help me-e-e-e. . . ."

Eric felt a shock of fear go through him.

Help me. Help me?

Vrrrt! The sound of stone grinding against stone filled the air. The back wall of the courtyard slid away and in its place stood a curtain.

A bloodred curtain.

"Maliban must be behind the curtain," said Keeah. "His voice is going through the statue."

Eric gasped as the curtain rippled from the spinning red wind.

"Maliban . . ." he murmured. "Maliban . . ."

Eric stared at the curtain and light flashed through his head. He closed his eyes. He saw a vision of the curtain and in his mind he walked up to it. He reached out his hand, grabbed the heavy cloth, and pulled it aside.

He staggered back.

What he saw terrified him. A face . . . that *wasn't* a face. It was something else. It was someone else. Someone Eric knew.

"What!" he cried. "It was you all the time!"

"Yes-s-s-s, Eric-c-c-c!" came the hissing reply.

Eric's eyes popped open. He turned to Keeah.

"The mask!" he said. "It's not for Prince Maliban."

Keeah stared at him. "What do you mean?"

"It's not for Maliban," Eric repeated, "because there *is* no Maliban."

Neal frowned. "Have you been eating the green part of the cheese again?"

"It's not Maliban behind that curtain."

"Then who is it?" asked Keeah. "Who?"

The red wind whoomed and boomed as it whipped higher around the statue. As it did, the silver statue itself turned red. The wind coiled higher and higher, nearing the golden mask.

The curtain rippled. The claw appeared.

Eric felt hot and cold at the same time.

But he knew he was right. He knew what his vision meant. Shaking his head firmly, he said, "There is no Maliban."

"Then who is it?" asked Neal.

Eric said a single word.

"Sparr."

Seven

The Magic in the Mask

Whooom! The dark storm of wind rose higher and higher.

As it did, the magic carpets flew around the statue. The boots danced and leaped, the bells rang, and the enchanted swords flashed and struck one another.

"Magic — enter the mask!" cried the voice.

Keeah turned to Eric. "What are you saying? It can't be Sparr. He's miles away from here. Galen saw him in his magic mirror."

Eric realized the time had come to reveal his secret. "Keeah, I have power, wizard power, and you gave it to me. Look."

He pulled the sleeves of his gown up. He showed them his hands. Blue sparks of electricity twinkled off the tips of his fingers.

"Whoa, awesome!" mumbled Neal.

"Not only that," said Eric. "I've been having, I don't know, *visions*, I guess you'd call them. I've been seeing glimpses of a monster. I've finally figured out who the monster is. It's him. Lord Sparr."

Keeah kept shaking her head. "But Galen . . ."

Eric remembered the old wizard tracing his finger over the mirror. "I'm sorry, Keeah, but Galen was . . . wrong."

The princess searched Eric's face. In that

half second, her eyes flashed with doubt, then surprise, then understanding. Keeah knew it, too. Galen *had* been wrong.

Whooom! The red wind spun faster.

"But why does Sparr need more magic?" said Neal. "He's the most power-ful sorcerer on Droon!"

"He *was* powerful," said Eric. "When the Golden Wasp stung him, he was hurt. Now he needs magic — all this magic — to get his own power back. Once Sparr wears Hob's mask — *shazam!* — he'll be his old nasty self again."

The red tornado of wind entered into the mask. It glowed a brighter red than ever.

Then one by one, the floating carpets flopped to the ground. The boots stopped jumping. The flying swords crashed down.

"The mask is stealing the magic!" said Keeah. "All the objects brought here are being drained of power. It's all going into the mask —"

"The power!" growled the voice. "Soon it shall be mine again!"

"We've got to free Julie," said Neal. "And get out of here. Galen was right about *one* thing. Tortu is a very bad place!"

Keeah turned to Eric. "We can do this. All of us. Together."

The look in her eyes was different from any Eric had ever seen before. She seemed frightened, but she looked at him as if she *knew* he could do this. And he felt it, too.

"You guys get Julie," he said. "I'll bring down the curtain. Show's over for this monster! Ready . . . go!"

Keeah charged ahead amid a shower of blue sparks. With one swift blast of her fingertips — *blam!* — she sent the guards stumbling away from Julie. Neal raced up and pulled her free.

"Guards-s-s, s-stop them!" The voice behind the curtain was more terrifying than ever.

But Eric was already moving across the courtyard. He raised his hands at the curtain, even as the bony claw pulled it closed.

Eric could hold it in no longer.

He leveled his hands at the curtain and spoke.

"*Kessa . . . moot . . . flah!*"

Instantly, a powerful blast of blue light shot out from his fingertips.

Kkkk-blam!

The curtain ripped in half. Its tatters flapped in the wind from the statue. And the thing behind it wriggled and slithered and clomped out into the light.

It was even more terrible than Eric's vision.

"Lord Sparr!" he yelled out.

"Yes-s-s-s-s!" was the hissing reply.

Neal fell backward. "Whoa! Talk about ugly! I'm Doofus the Handsome compared to him!"

Sparr was more monster than man.

His skin was speckled and dirty and pale, with dark scales over it. On his head were jagged, pointed ears. His spiky tail twitched across the floor. He turned his angry eyes toward Keeah.

"You!" he hissed. "Princess of Droon. It was you who made me this way."

Keeah stood her ground. "I set the Golden Wasp — your own evil creation — against you!"

"Yes-s-s-s! But after today, I shall be s-s-stronger than ever-r-r-r!" the sorcerer snarled. "It's s-s-so s-s-simple! The mask draws magic into it. When I wear it, I shall take all this power into mys-s-self."

Sparr stared at his twisted claws.

"And I shall be mys-s-self once more!"

Julie stomped her foot. "But yourself is so evil! How can you even stand it?"

"Being evil is the bes-s-st part," Sparr replied. "But look . . . the mask is ready!"

At that moment, the mask became unimaginably bright. The red wind — more like fire now — was entering into the mask, flooding its golden surface with a deeper red glow.

Sparr slithered over to the statue. Reaching up, he clutched the glowing mask.

"The power is mine —"

Boom! There was a sudden crashing sound from outside. The front gates blew off their hinges and a whirl of blue spun into the courtyard.

"Oh!" cried Hob. "Galen followed poor Hob!"

Sparr growled. "Galen! Can I *never* be rid of you?"

The good wizard's eyes showed an instant of surprise as his met the sorcerer's. "Sparr, you fiend, you shall not have the mask!"

With that, Galen sent a bolt of blue light hurtling from his hands.

KLA — BAMM!

The statue exploded and the golden mask skittered away from the sorcerer like a spinning top.

"Now we have you!" shouted Galen.

Another blue bolt of lightning burst at Sparr's feet, sending him tumbling away.

Sparr slithered back behind the tattered curtain and the wall closed behind him.

Galen rushed after him in a tornado of anger. "I shall stop you, Sparr!"

Instantly, the green guards charged at Galen. "Stop the wizard! Protect our master!"

As if angry with himself, the wizard

battled like a warrior half his age. He was everywhere at once! Hooded guards whooped and wailed as he tossed them aside with blast after blast.

In the confusion, Hob scurried out of the way and grabbed the glowing mask. "When wizards and sorcerers fight, poor little Hob takes flight!"

But he hadn't counted on one thing. Max. Seeing his master battling the guards so fiercely, Max leaped for Hob and tussled with him.

Hob growled and scrabbled with the spider troll but finally sent Max flying across the room — *splat*! Chuckling with glee, Hob pulled a carpet from the stack and plopped down on it.

"By the powers of ancient Goll, I command this carpet to fly!" he cried.

At once, the mask glowed and the carpet lifted. With one swift swoop, the imp flew up and over the wall of the courtyard, yelling, "Fly, carpet, fly!"

"Hob is escaping!" the wizard yelled, still battling the green guards. "We must get the mask. Hurry!"

"You heard the man," said Eric. "We've got a job to do!"

Eight

The Big Chase

Eric ripped off his blue gown and pulled Neal with him onto one of the lifeless carpets. He tugged on the fringe. The carpet just sat there.

"It's just a regular rug," said Neal. "The magic is all drained out of it —"

"We'll see about that!" said Eric. He tucked his legs beneath him, closed his eyes, and touched the rug with his hands.

Breathing deeply, Eric tried to find the quiet little room in his mind that Keeah had told him about.

Instantly, all the sounds of people yelling and running seemed to drift away. Eric felt peaceful and calm. And words — strange new words — sounded in his ears. He couldn't tell why or how he heard them, but he did.

And he spoke them aloud.

"Carpundem . . . sello . . . flee!"

Neal blinked at him. "What does that mean — whoa!"

The rug rose from the ground.

Eric opened his eyes and laughed. "I guess it means 'carpet up!' And now —" He pointed over the courtyard wall. *"Preddo . . . va!"*

"Can I quote you on that?" said Neal. "Yikes!"

With a sudden jerk, the carpet shot across the courtyard, skimming right over the heads of the green meanies.

"Hey, taxi! Wait for us!" Julie yelled as she, Keeah, and Max ran across the courtyard.

Eric circled overhead. "I've only been doing this for twelve seconds! I don't know the command for slow down! Or land! Or stop!"

"Then we'll just have to come up to you!" shouted Julie. She grabbed Keeah's hand, and with Max clinging to her back, she jumped.

Boing! Julie leaped out of the courtyard. A single bounce of her magic boots was all it took. They plopped right onto the flying carpet with Eric and Neal.

"Hold on tight, you guys!" Eric shouted. "We're in for a bumpy ride!"

Vooom! In a flash, they soared over the palace and out above the streets of the market.

Already Hob was rounding a far corner and entering the deep maze of shops and stalls, snorting and laughing the whole way.

"Oh, you want to race, do you?" said Eric. *"Ree-bo!"* he urged his carpet. It went faster.

"We'll have to go into the streets to catch him," said Keeah. "Better get down there."

Voom! They dove under an arch into a shop with magic swords dangling from the ceiling.

Swish! Clang! Slooop!

"Quickest haircut I ever got!" said Max, rubbing his orange hair. "There's Hob. Take a left!"

The fringes of Hob's carpet disappeared around a corner.

"Shortcut over the house!" said Julie, and Eric swooped the carpet up over a rooftop.

Faster and faster they flew, past shops, under arches, and bouncing down the narrow streets. But still Hob kept pulling away.

"All the magic in his mask is making the carpet faster," said Keeah.

"Don't worry, we'll catch him," said Eric. He felt the power surge through his body. It wasn't only in his fingers now but all through him. He felt more powerful than ever before.

"Oh, no!" cried Max, pointing to the tiniest of archways up ahead. "We'll never make it!"

"Tilt!" Neal urged. Everyone shifted

their weight and — *zooom!* — the carpet twisted sideways through the opening, with inches to spare.

"Good call, Neal," said Keeah.

He grinned. "Hey, I'm only Doofus the Ugly on the outside. On the inside, I'm Doofus the Smart. Now hit it, Erica!"

The five friends huddled close as the carpet swooped and soared. The cool night air rushed over them as they skimmed the rooftops.

And still Hob outflew them.

"The magic from the mask is too strong," said Keeah, the wind flying wildly through her hair.

Eric nodded. They snaked into one curving street and up between a fruit stall and its awning. They crashed through a string of hanging lights, scattering shoppers who shook their fists at the kids. But Eric wouldn't let up.

Finally, Hob yipped and yelled and soared over the city walls and out over the turtle's shell.

"Okay, now we can really fly!" shouted Eric.

"Except for that," said Neal. "What's that?"

A wall of black fog rolled across the darkening plains in front of them. And the turtle was approaching it.

"The Dark Lands!" said Keeah. "Tortu is entering Sparr's country. We're too close. Turn back."

"We can't stop now," said Eric, following Hob's every move even as he entered the fog.

Thick darkness rolled over the friends.

"Slow down at least," said Julie.

Eric gulped. "I sort of don't know how!"

The carpet bounced and dipped. It

tilted and sank. Heavy black air swam all around them.

"Are we up or down?" Neal coughed.

"I'm up," said Max, his voice trembling. "Now I'm down. Now I'm sliding off!"

Julie screamed. "Help, I'm falling!"

"We're going down!" yelled Keeah. "Eric, we're —"

Vooom — crash! The carpet slammed to the ground, scattering its riders across the turtle's hard shell.

Eric rolled and tumbled and slid until he stopped in a heap. Black smoke and fog whirled around him.

"Where am I?" he said, feeling dazed. He shook his head to clear it. "Keeah? Julie? Max? Are you there?"

There was no answer.

The fog was so thick and smoky, Eric felt as if he could hardly breathe. He struggled to his feet.

He could feel the turtle moving, but he didn't know which way to go. The gloom around him was as thick as night.

Then he heard a noise.

"Keeah?" he said. "Neal, is that you?"

Something slithered toward him across the shell. Then it clomped and thumped.

"Oh, no . . ." Eric backed away.

"Don't be afraid, Eric. It's-s-s only me-e-e-e!"

Nine

Welcome to the Dark Lands!

Eric's heart sank as the black air cleared and he saw the monster that was Lord Sparr.

"Welcome to my world," said the sorcerer.

Next to him was Hob, holding the glowing mask and grinning as if he were at a picnic.

"What do you want with me?" asked Eric.

"Much," said the sorcerer. "But first, you shall see what few have ever seen."

Sparr took the mask from Hob, the terrible glowing mask full of power, and clutched it tightly. "You shall see me become . . . *me!*"

Before Eric could move, the sorcerer pulled the golden face over his own monstrous features.

And he began to change.

His rough lizard skin shrank into the familiar black cloak. His front claws shriveled into pale bony hands, his hind legs into booted feet.

Sparr's face was hidden, but beyond the jutting horns of the mask poked the eerie fins that grew behind his ears.

"I . . . am . . . coming . . . back!"

As the sorcerer drew the power into himself, the mask's reddish glow dimmed. A moment later, the mask was no more than a dull gray piece of metal. It was Sparr himself who glowed.

Shimmering all over with the fiery light that had once been in the mask, Sparr stretched his arms and flexed his fingers. He seemed to ripple with new energy.

"Behold the power of me!" he said, laughing. Then, with a casual movement, Sparr tore off the mask and threw it to the ground.

"Hob did his job!" squeaked the imp. "Sparr shall pay him now!"

Laughing, the sorcerer tossed Hob a heavy bag of coins and Hob began to dance around.

It was then that Eric saw the red mark on Sparr's forehead. It was a jagged V-shaped scar left by the sting of the Golden Wasp so long ago.

"You know what?" said Eric. "You're still a monster. A crusty old wicked thing.

Somebody should stop you. Somebody will —"

"Ah, yes, but who?"

Eric felt his hands grow hot. His fingertips felt as if they could flash out at any second. He shook his head from side to side, his anger growing. "Galen will stop you."

"Galen!" Sparr spat out with a laugh. "His skills are failing. Have you noticed how *old* he looks? His enchantments are losing their power. He makes mistakes. Ah, well. It's because of where he was born."

Where he was born? What did Sparr mean?

Eric narrowed his eyes and gritted his teeth. He didn't want to hear that Galen was wrong. That he made mistakes. That he was getting old.

Sparr took a step toward Eric. "Soon, I shall overpower both Galen and the princess, and reclaim what is rightfully mine —"

"You won't!"

"I will," said Sparr. "And you — Eric Hinkle from the Upper World — you shall help me."

The words echoed in Eric's head.

Help me. . . .

Eric's blood boiled. "I'll never help you."

"You will find what I seek," said Sparr softly. "My spirit friend, Om, told you so. He said you will help me, and you shall. But you haven't told anyone about Om, have you? You like your small powers, don't you?"

Small powers?

"Well, then, it'll be our dark little secret."

Eric shivered. Every part of him was hot and cold at the same time. He felt his hands tremble. "The darkest thing here is your brain," he said.

Hob giggled. "The boy jokes with Sparr!"

Sparr stepped closer, but he wasn't laughing.

Eric's fingertips ached with a pain he had never felt before. But something else was happening, too. Even trembling, Eric felt . . . calm. He looked at Sparr and, though he was afraid, he knew what he had to do. To *try* to do.

"Tell me, Eric Hinkle," the sorcerer began. "Shall we be partners? Hmm? Yes or no? One simple word."

"The only word I have for you is . . . is . . ."

"Is what?" said Sparr, beginning to laugh.

Eric stared at the red mark on Sparr's forehead. His mouth opened.

"*Bubb . . . zee . . . doo!* Wait, that's not right —"

Suddenly — *splop! splop! splop!* — the air was filled with jelly doughnuts! They hung in the air for a moment, then — *thwack!* — they hurled themselves at the sorcerer!

Ploop! Splort! Plish!

They splattered Sparr's jet-black cloak with big drippy blobs of red jelly.

"Oh, Sparr likes that cloak," said Hob. "Boy has made a mess of it."

Sparr stopped laughing. He touched the jelly dripping down his cloak. His eyes flashed.

"So, you can do things, can you? Yes, you pass the test, Eric Hinkle, young wizard!"

Eric's mind was a blank. All he could think of were doughnuts and jelly and tiny birds.

Sparr went on. "Together, the two of us —"

"Wait! Did you say . . . together?"

Then, as if a soft familiar voice in Eric's head spoke the words, they came to him.

"*Septum . . . conda . . . ro!*"

"What! What?" the sorcerer sputtered.

But blue light had already left Eric's fingers.

K-k-k-k — blam!

The sorcerer fell back, staggering to the turtle's shell. The look on Sparr's face showed surprise.

"Who taught you that?"

Eric didn't bother to answer. Another blast shot from his fingertips. And another and another — *blam! blam! blam!* Sparr fell back farther, nearly stumbling to his knees.

"So I guess I failed your test!" said Eric.

"I AM LORD SPARR! SORCERER OF

GOLL!" Sparr bellowed. "Help me or not —
I shall teach you a lesson, you pip-squeak!"

Hob giggled and danced around. "Hob
likes that word! Funny word, pip-squeak!"

In a flash, Sparr rose up, towering over
Eric, fire spitting from his eyes, his fins
sharper and spikier than ever and turning
from red to purple to black.

From out of nowhere Sparr pulled a
jagged fireball the size of a basketball. But
it didn't stay that size for long. It grew
larger and redder and hotter until it seemed
the size of a small planet.

"Big ball of fire," said Hob. "Hob
doesn't like that so much!"

"Oh, y-y-yikes!" Eric stuttered. He fell
back, his hands sparking feebly. "Uh-oh!
Don't . . . please don't! You know, I can
really only do the doughnut trick. And
sometimes make erasers fly. But just for
a minute, then they fall. And there's the

chalk dust. It makes you cough. Really, I don't know much about anything —"

Sparr only laughed and launched the blazing fireball at Eric's head.

KLA-BAMMMM!

Ten

The End of Tortu's Tail

The explosion threw Eric hard to the turtle's shell. He felt sudden heat on his face. The sound of the fireball thundered in his ears.

Then there was nothing.

Eric opened his eyes.

Lord Sparr was rising away from him, spinning around and around in a funnel of black wind reaching up to the clouds. With a loud crackling noise, he vanished into the night sky.

Hob, his large eyes darting around, whimpered, then — *pop!* — he, too, disappeared.

Eric struggled to his feet. "Wow! Did I actually do that? I mean, I did do it! I actually did it!"

"Not quite," said a low voice behind him.

Eric swung around. Behind him stood the old wizard, his wrinkled hands stretched to the sky.

It was Galen who had saved him.

A moment later, Keeah, Julie, Max, and Neal came staggering out of the fog.

"So I *didn't* actually blast Sparr?" said Eric.

"You nearly got toasted and fried," said Julie.

"But the doughnuts *were* a good idea," added Keeah.

"Yeah," said Neal. "I hope the Dark Lands have washing machines. Sparr will need one for that cloak of his!"

"Come, children," said Galen. "While the sorcerer gathers his strength to strike again, we must find the turtle's tail. If Tortu enters the Dark Lands completely, we shall be lost, too. Hurry!"

With the wizard leading the way, the six friends took off toward the back edge of the shell.

The giant turtle seemed to pick up speed as they hurried along.

Finally, they burst through the ragged fog and came out under a twinkling sky.

"I see the tail!" said Julie. "Straight ahead."

At top speed, the six companions raced and jumped off the shell. They landed on the turtle's tail and ran down the length of it. When they got to the end, it flicked up and sent them flying.

Splat! Plomp! Wuff! Oomp! Eeee! Thwap!

They landed in the tall grass of the Thousand Mile Plains just as the tail — and the city of Tortu itself — vanished into the black air of Sparr's dark country.

"Tortu is gone," said Max. "Every bit of it."

"Even Julie's magic boots," said Neal.

Julie looked down at her bare feet. "Oh, man."

Suddenly — *flop! plop! clunk!* Three things fell to earth from where the turtle's tail had been. Two of them were Julie's sneakers. The third was small and red and rolled to a stop in the grass.

"The Ruby Orb of Doobesh," said Keeah.

"Ooh!" Max scrambled over to the ball. He picked up the glowing Orb. "Galen, may I have it to read by at night? Or to find what drops under my bed?!"

The wizard scanned the smoky air where the turtle had vanished, his brow furrowed in thought. "There is a reason the Ruby Orb remains. Let's bring it back to Jaffa City with us. Perhaps we can discover Sparr's plans."

Then the wizard sighed. "My friends, I was wrong about Sparr. My mirror is old. I am old."

"Ha!" Max protested. "You are the one who sent Sparr spinning away like a bad memory!"

Galen smiled sadly. "Perhaps, yes."

The evening lit up with a rainbow glow. The enchanted staircase was hovering over the grass nearby.

"I guess it's time," said Neal. "But I

don't want to go home. It was fun today. Mostly."

Eric knew the time had come for him to leave, too. When they reached the staircase, he turned.

"Galen, I'm sorry I didn't tell anyone I have powers. I just wanted them to last longer. It was fun having them. At least at first. But I've learned my lesson."

The wizard looked into Eric's eyes. "I knew from the moment you came today that you had powers. Five hundred years as a wizard gives one a sense of such things."

Eric held out his hands. The sudden light from his fingertips cast a blue glow on his face.

"Anyway," he said, "I shouldn't have powers. I got them by mistake. You can take them back."

"I cannot take them back!" Galen said,

his lips forming a smile. "No one can take them. And I do not believe you won the powers by accident. There is a greater purpose here."

Eric's mouth hung open. "Really? Whoa! But . . . there's something else."

In a rush, he told them everything that Sparr had said to him. About Eric helping him. What the spirit Om had told him. Everything.

Galen nodded. "So the mysteries deepen. My first job on returning to Jaffa City will be to delve into this new one. Ho-ho! There is never an end to mysteries and secrets in Droon!"

Keeah laughed. "I think you have powers, Eric, because you'll need them to be ready for Sparr. But between now and then, prepare to break a few things at home. My parents have a list of all the things I've broken."

"That list gets longer ever day!" said Max.

"Maybe next time you can give me some extra help?" said Eric. "I'm sure I'll need it."

"It's a promise," said Keeah.

They stood at the foot of the shining staircase.

"Bye, everyone," said Neal. "It's been so cool."

Julie nodded. "And very magical!"

When the three friends started up the stairs, Keeah stopped Eric. "One more thing," she said.

She held out her hand and a spark leaped between their fingers. Then silently, without moving her lips, Keeah spoke to him.

Can you hear me?

Eric blinked. *Wow! Yes. I can hear you!*

Then, no secrets, okay?

No secrets, he said. *Definitely.* At that moment, Keeah seemed closer to him than ever. He liked the feeling. Eric turned to his friends.

Neal? Julie?

"I hear you!" said Julie. "Wow!"

"Me, too," said Neal. "But don't start telling me secret jokes in class. I'll burst out laughing and get into big trouble!"

"That reminds me," said Eric. "There's a bunch of jelly doughnuts flying around my basement. If I don't make them vanish, *I'll* be in big trouble."

"Oh, we'll help with that," said Neal. "They can vanish right into my mouth!"

Saying good-bye, Eric and his friends ran up the stairs. He lit the way with his fingers.

As they turned one last time to wave to

their friends, Julie said, "Something tells me we'll be needed soon. Now that Sparr's back in action."

Neal nodded. "Yeah. But it's like Keeah said. We'll be ready for the guy."

Eric smiled to remember that moment when Lord Sparr — the great sorcerer himself — was covered in jelly.

"I like having powers," he said. *Plus, I'll be able to talk to you guys whenever I want!*

Neal wiggled his fingers in his ears. "That is truly weird. It's like you're right inside my head. This is going to take some getting used to."

Weird or not, Eric thought that it was good to be that close to his friends.

Closer than ever before.

Yes, it was very good.

"Come on," he said. "Let's go home."

When they reached the top of the stairs, Eric flicked his fingers, and the door to their world swung open, where their life — and three dozen flying doughnuts — were waiting for them.